This book belongs to:

_____

_____

 Berryland Books

Written by Gill Davies
Illustrated by Eric Kincaid
Edited by Heather Maddock

Published by Berryland Books
www.berrylandbooks.com

First published in 2004
Copyright © Berryland Books 2004

ISBN 1-84577-006-4
Printed in India

Little Red Riding Hood

Reading should always be FUN !

Reading is one of the most important skills your child will learn. It's an exciting challenge that you can enjoy together.

Treasured Tales is a collection of stories that has been carefully written for young readers.

Here are some useful points to help you teach your child to read.

Try to set aside a regular quiet time for reading at least three times a week.

Choose a time of the day when your child is not too tired.

Plan to spend approximately 15 minutes on each session.

Select the book together and spend the first few minutes talking about the title and cover picture.

Spend the next ten minutes listening and encouraging your child to read.

Always allow your child to look at and use the pictures to help them with the story.

Spend the last couple of minutes asking your child about what they have read. You will find a few examples of questions at the bottom of some pages.

Understanding what they have read is as important as the reading itself.

Once upon a time, there was a little girl who lived with her parents in a little house at the edge of the woods.

Her grandmother lived in a beautiful little house deep within the woods.

She really loved her granddaughter and enjoyed making her new clothes.

What did the grandmother like to make?

One day, when the little girl was visiting, her grandmother gave her a beautiful new cape.

It was made from red velvet and had a large hood.

The little girl liked it so much she wore it all the time.

From that day on, she became known as "Little Red Riding Hood".

Why was the little girl called Little Red Riding Hood?

One day, Little Red Riding Hood's mother said, "Your grandmother is not feeling very well, so I have put some things in a basket to cheer her up."

Little Red Riding Hood jumped up and said, "Please can I take it to grandmother?"

Her mother agreed and gave her the basket.

Little Red Riding Hood turned and waved goodbye to her mother.

Her mother called out to remind her not to talk to strangers on the way.

Little Red Riding Hood loved the woods.

She liked to skip along with the birds and butterflies.

Sometimes she'd stop and pick some flowers for her grandmother.

Where did Little Red Riding Hood like to skip?

Now, a wicked wolf who lived in the woods saw Little Red Riding Hood and licked his lips.

The wolf went up to Little Red Riding Hood and asked her where she was going.

"I'm going to see my grandmother," she said.

"She isn't feeling very well and my mother has packed this basket with some things for her," she continued.

Little Red Riding Hood then told the wolf exactly where her sick grandmother lived.

The wolf said goodbye and ran off into the woods.

The wolf thought of a wicked plan.

He took a short cut to the grandmother's house and knocked on the door.

Little Red Riding Hood's grandmother called out.

"Come on in, the door is open."

Who did grandmother think was at the door?

When grandmother saw the wolf she was very scared.

The wolf was about to jump on her. She leapt out of bed and ran for her life.

The wolf chased grandmother around the house.

Finally, the wolf got very tired and grandmother was able to escape.

She hid in the cupboard.

Where did grandmother hide?

The wolf put on grandmother's clothes.

He put on her spare glasses and climbed into her bed.

Then he lay waiting for Little Red Riding Hood to arrive.

Soon Little Red Riding Hood reached the house and went up to the door.

She was surprised to see that it was open and she called out to her grandmother.

No one answered, so she stepped inside and saw her grandmother lying in the bed.

Little Red Riding Hood thought her grandmother looked a bit strange.

"Oh grandmother, what large ears you have!" said Little Red Riding Hood.

"All the better to hear you with, my dear!" the wolf replied.

"Oh grandmother, what big eyes you have!" she said.

"All the better to see you with, my dear!" the wolf replied.

Little Red Riding Hood moved a little closer.

"Oh grandmother, what big teeth you have!" she said.

"All the better to eat you with!" said the wolf, and he leapt out of bed.

Little Red Riding Hood screamed.

As the wolf chased Little Red Riding Hood, she kept screaming for help.

A woodcutter working nearby heard her screams.

He rushed towards the little house with his axe.

The woodcutter saw the wolf chasing Little Red Riding Hood.

He raised his axe and with one swing he killed the wolf.

Little Red Riding Hood heard someone shouting.

She knew it was her grandmother.

She helped her grandmother out of the cupboard and gave her a huge hug.

"Thank you for rescuing my granddaughter," grandmother said to the woodcutter.

Where was Little Red Riding Hood's grandmother?

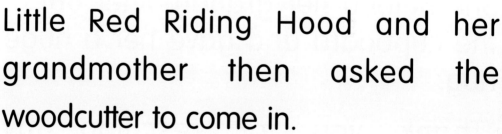

Little Red Riding Hood and her grandmother then asked the woodcutter to come in.

They all sat down to eat.

They emptied the basket and enjoyed the delicious cake with some tea.

"I'm feeling much better now," said grandmother to Little Red Riding Hood.

Little Red Riding Hood said goodbye to her grandmother, and then skipped all the way home.

Never again did she talk to strangers in the woods.